THE UNBELIEVABLE OLIVER

AND THE FOUR JOKERS

WRITTEN BY

PSEUDONYMOUS BOSCH

ILLUSTRATED BY

Shane Pangburn

To the Indomitable India and the Notorious Natalia –P.B.

For the Genuine Jennifer –S.P.

PUFFIN BOOKS
An imprint of Penguin Random House LLC, New York

First published in the United States of America by Dial Books for Young Readers
Published by Puffin Books, an imprint of Penguin Random House LLC, 2020

Text copyright © 2019 by Pseudonymous Bosch
Illustrations copyright © 2019 by Shane Pangburn

Visit us online at penguinrandomhouse.com

THE LIBRARY OF CONGRESS HAS CATALOGED THE DIAL EDITION AS FOLLOWS:
Library of Congress Cataloging-in-Publication Data
Names: Bosch, Pseudonymous, author. | Pangburn, Shane, illustrator.
Title: The Unbelievable Oliver and the Four Jokers / by Pseudonymous Bosch ;
illustrated by Shane Pangburn. | Description: New York : Dial Books for Young Readers, [2019] |
Series: [The Unbelievable Oliver ; 1] | Summary: "Eight-year-old aspiring magician Oliver and his rabbit
sidekick Benny must solve a mysterious robbery to save their act"— Provided by publisher. Includes directions
for performing a card trick. | Identifiers: LCCN 2019008253 | ISBN 9780525552321 (hardback) | Subjects: | CYAC:
Magic tricks—Fiction. | Rabbits—Fiction. | Birthdays—Fiction. | Parties—Fiction. | Robbers and outlaws—
Fiction. | Mystery and detective stories. | Humorous stories. | BISAC: JUVENILE FICTION / Mysteries &
Detective Stories. | JUVENILE FICTION / Fantasy & Magic. | JUVENILE FICTION / Humorous Stories.
Classification: LCC PZ7.B6484992 Un 2019 | DDC [Fic]—dc23
LC record available at https://lccn.loc.gov/2019008253

Puffin Books ISBN 9780525552338

Printed in the United States of America

1 3 5 7 9 10 8 6 4 2

Design by Jennifer Kelly
Text set in Adobe Text Pro

RUN OF SHOW

★ **INTRODUCTION** (quick opening trick) 1

Chapter One: Is This Your Card? 7

Chapter Two: The Gig 17

Chapter Three: Nothing Bunny About It 31

Chapter Four: Maddox's Birthday "Farty" 40

Chapter Five: The Grand Opening 52

Chapter Six: Showtime! 60

Chapter Seven: Accusations All Around 70

★ **INTERMISSION** (Bathroom Break) 83

Chapter Eight: The Who, the What, and the Where 85

Chapter Nine: The Investigation, Part One 94

Chapter Ten: The Investigation, Part Two 108

Chapter Eleven: Rabbit, Run 126

Chapter Twelve: Alibis, Alibis, Alibis 137

Chapter Thirteen: The Four Jokers 146

Chapter Fourteen: The Middle Name Drop 156

Chapter Fifteen: The After Party 168

★ **ENCORE** (How to Perform Oliver's Card Trick) 175

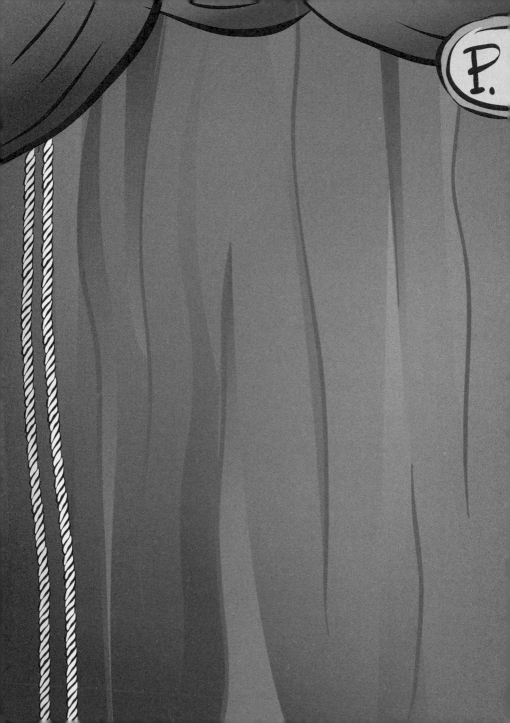

INTRODUCTION

Think of a number.

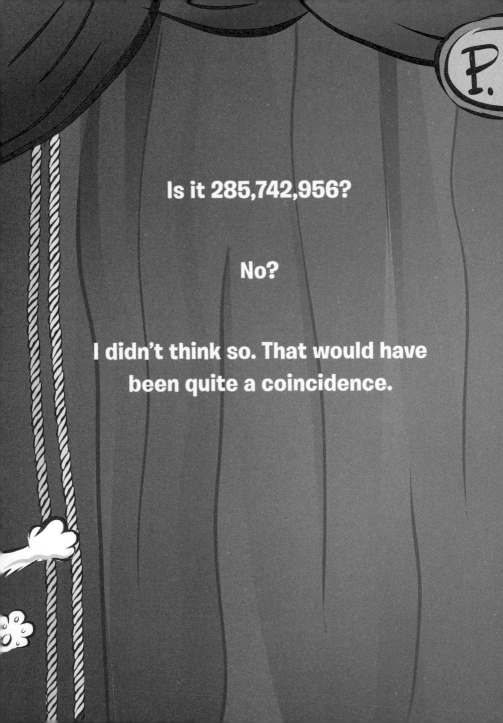

B.

Are you ready for some magic?

Today, I present a new work of illusion and mystery. It is a magic trick that I have been working on for many months.

I call it . . .

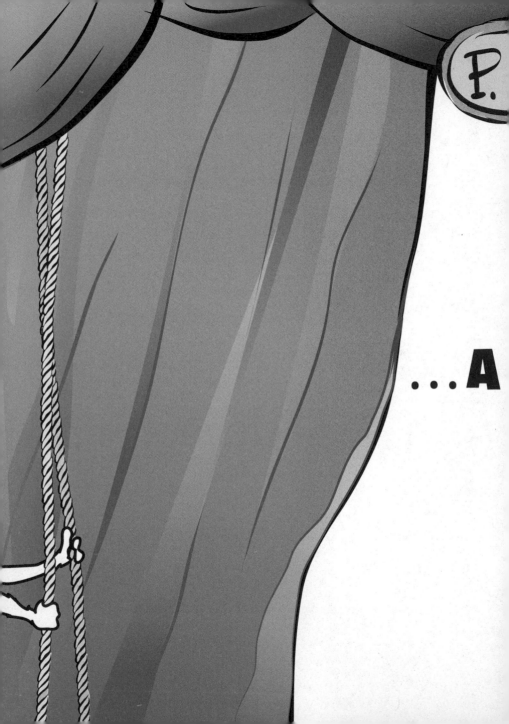

B.

BOOK!

All I need is
someone to read it.

Do I have
a volunteer?

1

Is This Your Card?

"Is this your card?"

It was not their card.

The twins, Bea and Teenie, short for Beatriz and Martina, were not impressed. They were even less impressed when the magician pulled another wrong card from the deck. Then another still . . .

"Is this your card?"

"Not that one either."

"Uh-uh."

"Come on!"

"No."

"Nope."

"Nah."

"No way!"

"That's from GO FISH!"

"That's *a fish*!"

sigh

Every card was wrong. Everything was wrong, really.

Oliver, our boy magician, was no wizard. He had no hat, no gloves, not even a wand. He was too small for his jacket, as well as for his age—eight last April. And he lacked the confidence you'd expect from anyone truly astonishing.

A magician should at least be astonishing. Wouldn't you agree?

He made one last effort to startle and amaze.

"Okay, is this your card?" he said, holding up the four of diamonds again.

"Yes!" said Bea.

"Maybe," said Teenie, who was having a little trouble paying attention. "See, we forgot our card. So it *could* be our card."

Oliver covered his face with the few remaining cards in the deck.

"Don't lie, Teenie!" Bea said with a glare.

"I'm not lying. I'm telling him the truth," Teenie insisted. "We forgot his card. *You* were lying."

"I lied to make him feel better. Don't you feel better, Oliver?"

Oliver did not feel better, but it seemed unkind to say so. He tried to smile, unsuccessfully.

"Maybe you're just not cut out to be a magician," said Teenie helpfully.

Oliver had only recently started dabbling in the magical arts, after borrowing a deck of cards from his cousin Spencer, who worked at the local magic shop. Several cards were missing from the deck, but it had "all the main ones," Spencer had assured him. "Anyway, you don't need a full deck for most tricks. You'll see, magic is easy."

Oliver was beginning to think his cousin had misled him.

"Thank you for inviting me to your tea party," said Oliver. "You said there was going to be cake."

If there was one thing that was going to make Oliver feel better, it was cake.

"You're welcome, Oliver," Bea replied. "The cake is right in front of you—it's imaginary. Like the tea. Do you want to play Genius Fairies?"

Oliver loved cake. All kinds of cake. Cupcake. Sponge cake. Pancake.

He even loved imaginary cake. Most days, it was the only sort of cake that his mother, who was a health food nut, would let him have.

He did not love Bea's current favorite make-believe game, Genius Fairies: magical fairies who were good at math and science. Not Oliver's strongest subjects.

Before he could refuse to play, Teenie chimed in: "Frida doesn't want to play Genius Fairies. She wants to play Super Fairies." Super Fairies were good at running, sneaking, and acrobatics. Also not Oliver's strongest subjects.

"Her name's not Frida." Bea pointed to the cat. "It's Calico."

"Frida!"

"Calico!"

As the girls fought, Oliver checked the cat's collar.

ACHOO!

In all the excitement, Oliver forgot that he was allergic to cats.

"Oliver, did you get an invitation to Maddox's party?"

Oliver was relieved that they had changed the topic. But not so relieved when he realized what the new topic was.

Maddox, the richest kid at Nowonder Elementary, was turning nine that Saturday. His party was the talk of the third-grade class.

"Um . . . it must have gotten lost in the mail," Oliver said. "It's okay, I can't go anyway."

"You have to go—he has a pool!" Bea declared. "Besides, if we don't go to the party, Maddox will think that we don't like him."

"Wait. We don't have a present," said Bea. "If we don't bring a present, then he'll really know we don't like him."

"What can *we* get Maddox?" Teenie asked. "Wait. Does he have a cat?"

"I'm not giving him Frida!" said Bea.

"You call her Calico!"

"Well, I'm not giving him Calico either."

"What then?"

Teenie and Bea looked at each other, then together they yelled at the top of their lungs: "Daddy! Papa! Emergency! We have to go to the pet store!"

Forgetting about Oliver, they ran upstairs to talk to their fathers.

Left alone at the table, Oliver turned to Frida/Calico.

IS **THIS** YOUR CARD?

The Gig

Do you know the expression that begins, *If at first you don't succeed . . . ?* As far as Oliver was concerned, it ended . . . *do not humiliate yourself again.*

After the tea party fiasco, Oliver decided he was not cut out to be a magician. (*Fiasco* is a very useful word; it means disaster. I find there can never be enough words for disaster.) He would have to look for a new occupation. Baker maybe? He liked cake, after all. He could see his business card already:

Or did "Kid Baker" make it sound as if he were baking kids instead of cakes?

The next day, Oliver's mother was working late, so he got a ride home with Bea and Teenie.

As always, he got the middle seat, but because he had a generous spirit he didn't complain. Also, it was the only way his booster seat fit.

Usually, the middle seat put him in the middle of a fight between the twins, with Bea angrily complaining that it was too loud for her to read and Teenie noisily humming and tapping on the window. Today, the twins were in agreement, which was worse.

"Great news! We got you invited to Maddox's party," Teenie said.

"I wish you hadn't," said Oliver, distressed. "Did he know he was inviting *me*?"

"Well, no," Bea admitted. "But don't worry, you're not really invited. More like . . . booked."

"Booked?"

"Exactly," said Teenie. "It's a paid gig."

"It is? Wait. What's a gig?"

Bea tapped a drumroll on her book. "You're the entertainment!"

"You'll be doing a magic show!" Teenie sang. "Isn't that amazing?"

"But I'm not a magician!" Oliver protested. "Besides, I told you, I have Hebrew school."

"Maddox's birthday is Saturday. You have Hebrew school on Sunday," said Bea, who knew Oliver's schedule better than he did. "Anyway, you can't back out. We promised Maddox. He's expecting the greatest magician this side of the Mississippi."

"M-i-s-s-i-s-s-i-p-p-i," Teenie whispered. Having just learned to spell *Mississippi,* she could not think of the name without also spelling it.

"So you see, this isn't really about you, Oliver," Bea added. "It's about our honor. You can't besmirch our honor."

Oliver didn't know what *besmirch* meant, but it sounded very bad.

What could he do? He wasn't a real magician. He wasn't even a real *kid* magician.

"I've never performed in front of a crowd," he said. "I've never even done an oral report."

"It's easy," Bea said. "Just imagine they're all cats."

"Or in their underwear," Teenie added.

Oliver did his best to imagine
cats in underwear.

"Anyway, you have plenty of time to practice,"
said Bea. "The party isn't till tomorrow."

That's twenty-four hours, thought Oliver. He
couldn't possibly learn magic in twenty-four
hours. He couldn't even learn his multiplication tables in that time. To be
honest, he didn't think he'd ever
learn his multiplication tables.
He was in a panic.

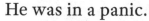

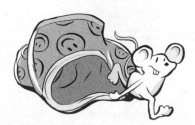

Here are some ideas about what to do when you're in a panic:

1 Practice your multiplication tables:

2 Make up a mantra. Repeat it until someone makes you stop:

3 Hide your head in your shirt and disappear:

4 Address the problem:

In the end, Oliver could think of only one thing to do. And it wasn't so much a thing to do as a place to go.

The Great Zoocheeni's Magic Emporium did not look very magical. It looked cluttered and dirty. The first time he'd visited, Oliver had been very disappointed. This was the second time he'd visited, and he was still disappointed. On the shelves were the same dusty magic sets, the same used how-to DVDs, the same faded rubber chickens.

"Hey, cuz," Spencer said without looking up from his phone. "Don't tell me, you want a plastic poop. I told you nobody falls for those."

"I need magic lessons, and a hat, and a wand," Oliver said in a rush. "And how much do rabbits cost?"

"Slooooooow down." Spencer rose from the stool behind the counter. He was tall and slim and had taken to wearing suspenders. "Let's start with the hat."

Oliver surveyed the hats, all well out of his price range, which was the five dollars he'd saved by not buying lunch two days this week, meatloaf Monday (yuck) and vegetable soup Tuesday (gross).

"What can I get for five dollars?" Oliver asked.

"Zero hats," said Spencer. "But tell you what, there's an old hat in the back that we were going to throw away. A man came from Las Vegas last week. Sold everything, even his cape."

Spencer tossed Oliver an old, moth-eaten top hat. It was so heavy that he fell to the ground catching it. The hat was velvet, and was once maybe blue or possibly purple. What it had lost in color it had gained in smell.

"Did somebody puke in this?"

"Not lately."

The hat fit like a glove. A glove that was much too large.

"It looks great on you," Spencer said as he took a picture of his cousin.

Spencer
Zoocheeni's Magic Emporium

4 likes

$pen¢er: I told my little cousin the hat looks great

"What about magic lessons?" asked Oliver.

Oliver took off the hat and placed it on the counter. The hat appeared to move ever so slightly toward the candy dish near the cash register.

That's impossible, Oliver thought. Even a magician's hat doesn't move on its own.

"Zoocheeni stopped giving lessons," Spencer said. "Not enough money in it."

"But I need to learn magic for a birthday party tomorrow! It's a paid gig—"

At the sound of "paid gig" a flash of smoke filled the room, followed by a coughing dove and the Great Zoocheeni himself.

"Magic can't just be taught, my boy." Zoocheeni spoke with his wand in the air as if he were conducting an orchestra. "It has to be lived. Believe, and your audience will follow."

Oliver could not follow. He was distracted by the dove, who had perched on Oliver's new hat and was pecking at the brim. The hat appeared to peck back.

"And how much are they paying for this 'gig,' as you call it?" Zoocheeni continued. "This 'burrrth-day partay.'"

The great magician said "birthday party" as if it were something quite smelly, like a sock worn a second day or a used magician's hat. The dove pinched her beak in revulsion.

"I'm not sure," Oliver replied. "They have a lot of money, though. He's got a pool."

"A pool, you say?" Zoocheeni rubbed his chin in thought. "How very interesting. Aboveground or . . . Never mind. Such trifles are beneath me. As are birthday parties. You asked for a magic lesson. How much are *you* willing to pay?"

"Five dollars."

Oliver was proud of his five-dollar bill and held it in the air. The dove snatched it and dropped it into the open cash register.

Zoocheeni nodded to the dove. "Thank you, Paloma," he said in a voice full of adoration.

The magician turned back to Oliver. "For five dollars, I couldn't teach you a single trick."

"But Mr. Zucchini! The dove—"

The magician rose to his full height. "How dare you call me that! It's Zoo-*cheeni*. Like zoo-cheesy. But with an *n*!"

"I'm sorry," said Oliver desperately. "But the dove took my money. Can't you at least teach me one trick?"

Zoocheeni considered. "Well, maybe just one. . . ."

Oliver was excited to learn a new trick, but before he could take out his notepad and pencil, he was picked up by the scruff of his neck and thrown out the door.

"What about the trick?" he called out.

"That was it," came the answer. "I taught you to disappear!"

Oliver's new hat came sailing after . . .

with a  CLANK

a THUMP,

two hops, and a GROAN!

Nothing Bunny About It

Oliver sat in the alley behind the magic store, wishing he could disappear altogether. What was he going to do? He was supposed to do a magic show, and all he had was a smelly hat and no tricks.

"Psst."

Oliver looked around.

"Anybody out there?" asked a gruff voice.

Psst...

Oliver looked around again. He couldn't see anybody.

"Just me," he said. "And . . . you?"

"Oh, I'm here all right. Why else would my tush hurt so much?"

Oliver nodded uneasily. "Are you sure you're not just in my head?"

"Well, I was *on* your head a moment ago. But now I seem to be out on the street. Not that it's the first time, mind you."

Oliver looked around yet again, until his eyes fixed on the top hat. It moved a little.

Slowly, recognition dawned. "You're a . . . hat?"

"What? Ha! Now that would be a first!"

A head popped out of the hat. "No, this here is just my crib, my pad, my castle, *mi casa*."

Oliver stared.

It was the head of a rabbit. The head of a rabbit wearing sunglasses.

"Thanks for busting me out, kid. You did me a solid."

"You're welcome," said Oliver, more than a little bit confused.

The rabbit looked around suspiciously, sniffed. "And here I thought I knew every back alley in Vegas." He shrugged. "So can you tell me how to get to the Luxor?"

"Isn't Luxor a city in Egypt?" asked Oliver.

"No, kid. It's a hotel in Vegas. Why, does Egypt have pyramids too?"

Oliver nodded his head. "But we're not in Egypt. Or Vegas."

"This isn't Vegas? Is it Reno? I can't go back to Reno! Not without a disguise." The rabbit eyed the back door of the magic shop as if his enemies were about to walk out of it. "Can you spare me a disguise? On second thought, can you loan me a Hamilton?"

"A Hamilton?"

"A ten, kid. No? Okay, make it a Lincoln. A fiver. Any green at all?" The rabbit's eyes narrowed. "And no, I don't mean carrot tops, wise guy. Trust me, I've heard all those jokes before."

"The Great Zoocheeni took my money," said Oliver nervously. "I won't have any more until I get paid for the magic show."

"Magic show! Why didn't you say so? I know a thing or two about magic. What tricks you got up your sleeve, kid?"

Oliver didn't know any tricks.

"Let me get this straight," the rabbit said as he returned Oliver's nose. "You don't even know the Four Jacks? It's the oldest trick in the book! Also known as the Four Kings. Four Queens. Or Four Whatever Card You Want to Use."

"My deck doesn't have four of any card," said Oliver. "Except jokers. And I think they come from different decks."

The rabbit twitched his nose in dismay. "And yet you say you're a magician?"

"No . . ."

"Well, not with *that* attitude, you aren't! You got a gig, though, huh?"

Oliver nodded glumly. "A birthday party."

"Birthday? I haven't worked a birthday party in years. All those little monsters pumped up on sugar and running wild—no thank you. Still, you could do worse than to talk to me."

"Wait, you can talk!" Oliver only then realized he'd been chatting with a woodland creature for several minutes.

"Yeah, kid, whadya think I've been doing? So, whose birthday is it? How many invited? Any wise guys?"

"It's Maddox's birthday party. It'll be a big party. He invited the whole class. Except me."

"Ah, so we're sneaking in the side door, are we? That'll teach 'em." The rabbit nodded approvingly. "What's the take?"

Oliver shrugged. He didn't know what *the take* meant.

"The money, kid. The haul."

"Oh!" Oliver said. "A lot, I think. He has a pool."

"A pool, huh?" The rabbit thought it over. "Aboveground or . . . Never mind—let's cut to the chase. It just so happens that I have a little leisure time right now. And there's these guys in Reno who, well, I could use the dough. Know what I'm saying?"

Oliver had no idea what the rabbit was saying, but he nodded anyway.

"Good, good, I knew you had to be sharper than you seemed," said the rabbit enthusiastically.

"What do you say we go partners on this birthday business. We split it Even-Steven, right down the middle. Sixty-forty. Give me a paw."

Oliver was pretty sure that an even split would be fifty-fifty. Then again, he wasn't very good at math. He extended his hand.

"What's your name again, kid?" the rabbit asked.

"Oliver."

"I'm gonna call you Ollie."

"I'd rather you didn't," Oliver said. "What's your name?"

"Well, Ollie, I'm Benny."

"As in *bunny*?" Oliver laughed.

"No, as in Benny." The rabbit turned his back on

the boy. "Nothing bunny about it. Nothing funny, either, Ollie . . . Wait. What do you call yourself?"

"I just told you: Oliver." Oliver was beginning to think that this talking rabbit was a bit nuts.

"No, no, your stage name, kid. You can't be a magician without a stage name. You know, the Amazing . . . the Magnificent . . ."

"Oh." Oliver had actually given this a little bit of thought. "I was thinking, maybe, the Great Oliverini?"

The rabbit shook his head. "Unbelievable."

"You're saying that should be my name?" Oliver struck a magical pose. "The Unbelievable Oliver!"

Benny covered his sunglasses with a paw.

THIS IS GONNA BE A **DISASTER.**

Maddox's Birthday "Farty"

Oliver lived only a few blocks away, but Maddox may as well have lived on a different planet. A planet with greener grass, cleaner roads, and, Oliver suspected, meaner residents.

A guardhouse and gate blocked the entry to Maddox's street. You had to say a password just to drive in.

The password was "Maddox's Party." Bea and Teenie made their papa practice first.

"Try to act cool about it," said Bea. "Don't let the guard know that you're nervous."

"I'm not nervous," their papa said.

"Just say something like, We're here for MAD-DOX'S PARTY," said Teenie, winking.

"*Estamos aquí para la fiesta de Maddox,*" said their papa, winking back.

"*En ingles!*" said the twins, giggling.

(Even though his grandparents came from Mexico, their papa did not grow up speaking Spanish—a grave misfortune he tried to make up for by speaking the language with his daughters whenever he could.)

"And don't wink!" added Bea.

Teenie, Bea, and Oliver were crowded in the backseat along with Bea's backpack and Maddox's gift, which was decorated with a drawing of what might or might not have been a flying cat.

"It's a Robo-Kitty Deluxe II," Teenie whispered to Oliver. "A robot cat! But don't tell anybody."

Oliver had nobody to tell, except maybe Benny, who'd already heard everything, since he was hiding in the hat atop Oliver's head. The rabbit tried to be quiet but couldn't help farting occa-

sionally. The car was starting to smell as they arrived at the guardhouse.

"Who's doing that?" asked Bea, looking at Oliver.
Oliver smiled weakly.

"We're here for Maddox's *farty,*" said Papa to the
guard.

Everyone laughed—even the guard, who waved them in, and at the same time waved away the smell.

Benny lifted the hat slightly and whispered to Oliver:

WHAT'S SO FUNNY?

"What do you have under there?!" asked Bea in alarm.

"Where?" Teenie asked.

Bea pointed to the hat. "It moved!"

"Tell them it's dandruff," Benny whispered to Oliver. "Or lice."

But Teenie was too quick. She lifted Oliver's hat, revealing Benny's twitching nose. "There's a rabbit on your head!"

Bea stared in disbelief. "Wow. It's almost like you're a real magician!"

"Almost," Oliver said, nervously readjusting his hat. "But keep it secret. Benny, er, the rabbit is the big finale."

He and Benny had agreed that the rabbit should appear only briefly. And should never, ever speak in front of others. No need to raise questions.

They could tell which house was Maddox's right away. It was the biggest in a row of already big houses, and it had the fanciest cars parked in front. Also, it was decorated with big balloon letters spelling M-A-D-D-O-X.

Bea and Teenie entered the party, holding Maddox's present between them because they both wanted credit for bringing it.

Oliver followed, holding his stomach because it was turning over and over like a washing machine.

"Are Maddox and his friends talking to a clown?" asked Bea when she was done marveling at the height of the entry room's ceiling.

The birthday boy was standing next to his three very unfriendly friends, Joe, Jayden, and Memphis. This was not surprising. Maddox was almost never *not* standing with them. What *was* surprising was that he was also standing next to a man with a bright red nose and a big curly wig—and, mysteriously, a cape. (As a rule, clowns don't wear capes.) On

the man's shoulder was a white bird, also wearing a clown nose.

Oliver thought he recognized them, but from where he couldn't remember. Thankfully, he didn't know any clowns.

Maddox's mother approached.

"Mom, tell him to go home!" Maddox shouted. "I don't want some pathetic clown!"

"I'm so sorry. I must have the wrong burrrthday partay," said the clown, sounding not at all sorry.

He swung his cape around in a very un-clown-like fashion. The bird swung its wing in the same way. Then they brushed past Oliver and exited the premises.

Maddox grabbed Teenie and Bea's gift with barely a glance, then dumped it off on his big friend Joe, who did all of Maddox's heavy lifting.

Maddox's mom smiled apologetically at Bea and Teenie. "That wasn't your magician, was it? *The Unbelievable Oscar*?"

"Oliver," Oliver mumbled.

"Oh, so *you're* Oscar?" said Maddox's mother. "Wonderful."

Maddox glared. "What's *he* doing here?!"

"Now that's not very nice," Maddox's mother chided. "This young man is a professional magician. And we've asked him to do a show! Won't that be fun?"

Maddox's response made it clear that he did not think it would be fun.

He appeared to be throwing a tantrum, but of course that was impossible, as this was his ninth birthday and nine was far too old for tantrums.

Eventually, it was decided that Oliver could stay and do the magic show. In return, Maddox would get to open presents first.

Benny, for one, was relieved. "We're in, kid!" the rabbit shouted from inside the hat. "Getting in is always the hardest part. Except for getting out."

Bea looked suspiciously at Oliver. "Did you say something?"

"Just my stomach. I'm nervous about the show." That much was true at least.

"Everyone, change of plan," Maddox's mother announced. "Please come to the den."

On their way into the party, all the third graders of Nowonder Elementary had been handed maps of the premises.

What's the difference between a den and a living room? Oliver wondered as he checked his map.

The Grand Opening

Soon the whole third grade was gathered in the den, watching Maddox tear through a mountain of gifts while a football game played silently on the giant screen behind him. (To judge by Maddox's house, a den was basically a living room with a big TV—so big, in this case, that it took up an entire wall.)

Just like at school, Maddox sat in the middle of the room, flanked by his flunkies: Memphis, Joe, and Jayden.

"Clothes! Gross," he said, shaking a big box. "What am I supposed to do with those?"

He tossed the box aside, unopened.

Oliver watched from the patio outside. Judging by the dwindling pile of presents, he had only minutes to prepare for his show.

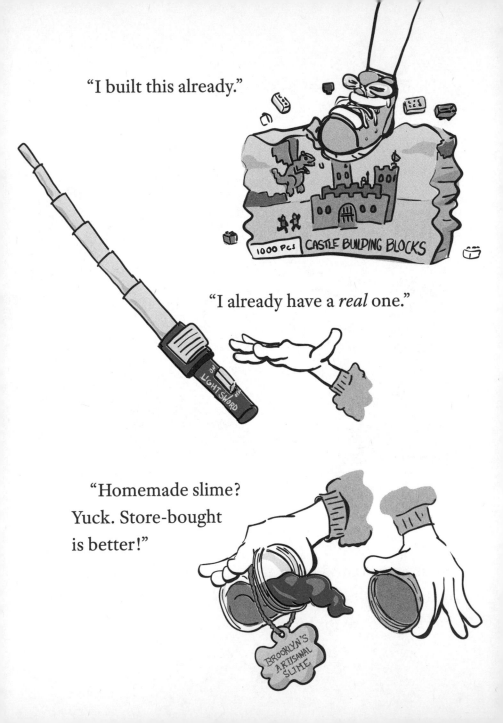

As Maddox rejected one gift after another, his friends cheered and jeered.

Nearby, a housekeeper gathered the torn wrapping paper and misplaced birthday cards.

"We need those so we can send thank-you notes later," Maddox's mother explained. Maddox had never written a thank-you note in his life, but she remained optimistic.

Finally, only the gift from Bea and Teenie was left. Maddox eyed the flying cat drawing with disdain. "Who drew that? It looks like it's for a girl."

"Maddox!" scolded his mother.

"Whatever." He picked up the gift, about to toss it away.

"Meow!" said the gift.

"What the—" Suddenly interested, Maddox ripped open the package.

"Whoa! Finally, something good. An RK-D2! Cooooool."

MEOW

"Oh!" At this change in attitude, Maddox's mother's ears perked up. "Who was that from?"

"Who cares?" Maddox said. "It's mine now."

Bea raised her hand. "We got him the RK-D2. Me and Teenie. And Oliver . . . kinda."

"Thank you, girls." Maddox's mother smiled at the twins. "Maddox, don't you want to thank Beatriz and Martina and Oliver . . . kinda?"

"Thank you, oh thank you, Beatriz and Martina and Oliver . . . kinda," said Maddox in a tone some might call sarcastic. (Others might call it mean.) "But nobody else!"

"I was going to get him that," Memphis whispered to Teenie, who pretended not to hear.

Through the sliding glass doors, Oliver could see that the present pile had disappeared. It was almost showtime.

"Focus, kid," Benny shouted from inside the hat. "It's great that you're doing your breathing exercises, but focus!"

Oliver wasn't doing breathing exercises. He was hyperventilating.

FOCUS!

"I'm sorry," Oliver said. "I'm trying."

They'd been drilling the same simple trick for the last five minutes, but Oliver wasn't getting it.

"Maybe it works better if you're a rabbit," said Oliver.

Maddox's mother approached to see the young magician talking to his hat.

"Is that part of your mystique, talking to a hat? A magician has to have mystique."

"What?" asked Oliver, startled.

"It's time for the show," said Maddox's mother. "You better rub your lucky rabbit's foot."

"You better not!" came the instant reply from inside Oliver's hat.

Maddox's mother smiled uncertainly. "Are you sure you're ready?"

Oliver was not ready.

Showtime!

For Oliver's show, the patio had been outfitted with red velvet curtains, a blinking neon sign, and rows of folding chairs that now contained the entire third-grade class, excluding Oliver. Twenty-four kids. All staring at him with varying degrees of disinterest and suspicion.

It was like looking at his class photo, which he'd also been excluded from. (Well, not exactly excluded, just blocked by a few taller kids.)

Benny paced nervously on top of his head.

"Okay, Ollie, this is it—showtime!" the bunny whispered in his ear. "Years of practice and preparation, sweat and tears, and it all comes down to this one moment. Weaker souls would crumble at a time like this. But you—well, I know you, and what I know about you . . . well, it's not a lot, honestly."

In front of Oliver was a microphone on a stand.

He'd never used a microphone before and he didn't want to use one now, but Bea and Teenie had requested it.

"It's part of your rider," Bea said. "Along with four pieces of birthday cake."

Oliver wasn't sure what a rider was, but it seemed to impress Benny. "Next time, have them ask for carrots—a dozen, and by a dozen, I mean thirteen, a bunny's dozen," the bunny specified.

Magician's Rider
THE UNBELIEVABLE
OLIVER

• Cake
  4 slices
  corner preferred

• Microphone & stand

• Sparkling Water
  (RoomTemp!)

For his part, Oliver was happy just to have four pieces of cake.

"Two slices are for us," Teenie clarified.

The mic stand was too tall. Oliver lowered it as far is it would go, which was still a full foot over his head.

"That's great, kid." Benny pawed at Oliver's scalp. "You've got 'em laughing. Now hit 'em with another joke."

Oliver couldn't remember any jokes. The microphone "joke" had not been intentional.

Sensing that he needed encouragement, Bea stood up. "And now, ladies and gentlemen, let's give it up for the Unbelievable Oliver!"

She started clapping madly. Nobody joined her except Teenie and Rose, another class outcast, who was always wearing cat ears. Oliver had been a little surprised to see her at the party. If even Rose was invited, what must Maddox think of *him*?

Luckily, the sight of Rose reminded Oliver to think about cats in underwear. It helped a little. He forced himself to speak.

"Thank you," he said. "Today Maddox is nine years old. That's old, huh? I'm still eight. Say, what did Zero say to Eight? Anyone?"

"Nice belt?" Teenie chimed in.

"Why thank you, it's new." Oliver bowed to the

total silence of the crowd. "Get it? The middle of the eight is the belt."

Oliver swallowed. "So who's ready for some magic?"

Nobody spoke up. Rose tentatively raised her hand, then dropped it. Oliver proceeded anyway.

"I need a volunteer. Anyone? You, young man." He pointed to Maddox, who responded with a dead stare.

"I'm going to go play with my robo-cat," Maddox said, and ran toward the kitchen.

But it's your birthday, Oliver thought, paralyzed. This show is for you.

"Never mind him," Benny whispered. "Just keep talking. Silence is the enemy. Skip to the French Drop if you're stuck."

Oliver gathered his courage to continue. "Do you by chance have a quarter, Mrs. Maddox's Mom?"

Maddox's mother gamely handed the young magician a quarter. He displayed it with a flourish, before attempting to pinch it in his right hand.

1 Press coin between thumb
and forefinger.

2 Use your thumb to lift the coin
up and over your knuckles.

3 "Accidentally" drop the coin.

4 Don't panic.

5 Cover the coin with
your shoe.

"And *voilà,* it's gone!"

In the rush of motion, he dropped the coin.

"As you can see, the coin has . . . d-disappeared," he stammered. "But I'm no burglar. That was your quarter and you deserve it back."

Oliver had no way to get the quarter off the ground without being noticed. "Hey, Benny," he said under his breath. "Do you have a quarter?"

"Sure thing, Ollie," Benny whispered back. "You're gonna have to pull me out of the hat, though. You up for it?"

Oliver didn't feel up for anything. Nonetheless, he lifted the hat from his head.

"I always keep spare change in my hat." Oliver offered the hat to Maddox's mom. "Check and see."

Benny hid under the hat's false bottom as she reached for the coin.

"There's nothing there." She seemed disappointed.

"Are you sure?" Oliver reached in the hat, and pulled Benny out by his ears, the coin clenched between his massive incisors. "Ta-da!"

For the first time, the audience began to clap, but they were quickly silenced.

"Stop!" Maddox shouted. Everyone's head swiveled as the birthday boy returned. "Nobody move. Mom, call the police. There's been a robbery."

"Did he say *police*?" whispered Benny through his clenched teeth. "I knew this gig was too good to be true."

"But the rabbit was just about to give the quarter *back*," Maddox's mom said.

At this, the rabbit nodded vigorously, dropped the quarter to the ground, and swung himself head-first back into the hat.

"Not the quarter," said Maddox, kicking the coin away. "The robo-cat. RK-D2. I left it right on top of the kitchen island, and it's gone."

He looked accusingly at his classmates. "Somebody here stole it!"

Accusations All Around

Now, I like magic as much as the next person who writes books about magic and thinks about magic all day long. But, forgive me, there is something that sometimes fascinates me more than a magic trick.

Chocolate? Yes, of course, chocolate always comes first. However, I'm thinking of something else at the moment.

Crime.

In my fascination with crime I am not alone. As soon as Maddox uttered the word *robbery,* every guest at his party was transfixed. Forget about Oliver's magic show. A theft—now that was interesting!

You could have heard a pin drop, never mind a quarter from a rabbit's mouth.

Maddox's mother tried to remain calm. "Now, Maddox, be reasonable," she said to her son. "Who would steal a cat?"

All eyes turned to Rose, who paled under her cat ears.

"Rose must have taken it," said Jayden. "She's way too into cats."

Rose was, in fact, very much into cats. Aside from the cat-ears headband, she wore a cat T-shirt, a cat backpack, and more cat hairs than you could count.

"I didn't take the cat," Rose said. "I'm allergic."

"But you love cats!" Memphis shouted. "You're the weird cat girl!"

Rose stood her ground. "Oh, I love cats. I'm allergic to *robots*."

Her classmates made skeptical noises. They knew about a lot of allergies, but this was a new one.

"I'm serious." Rose lifted her arm to show her medical wristbands. "See?

"It's the silicon. That's why I don't use computers."

Suddenly, the weird cat girl's behavior began to make more sense.

"It was Oliver then," Memphis said. "He makes things disappear."

"No I don't!" Oliver looked around for something that might prove his point, but Benny was hiding inside the hat, and the coin Maddox had kicked was nowhere to be seen.

Maddox turned to the partygoers. "He's trying to trick us! But it won't work. We aren't falling for it this time."

Bea tried to help. "Oliver isn't a good enough magician to pull off that kind of disappearing act."

"Or maybe the twins took it," Memphis said. "They wanted the RK-D2 for themselves."

"That's not true!" Teenie shouted. "We wanted the calico model."

Maddox nodded, an unpleasant smile on his face. "Yeah, that's why they got me the cat! Think about it. Their mom won't buy it for them, so they had her buy it for me. Then they stole it back."

"But we don't have a mom," Teenie said.

THE RABBIT
TOOK IT!

ROSE!

BROOKLYN!

AUSTIN!

"So your dads got it for you." Maddox shrugged. "Same thing."

Jayden joined in: "It's the perfect alibi! Nobody would suspect you."

"Yeah," said Joe. "Not even us!"

Even though they were wrong about the twins, Oliver had to admit the mean kids were smarter than he'd thought. Their logic was sound.

"Maybe it's just lost," Oliver suggested.

"Maybe *you* lost it, loser!" said Maddox. "Or more like you took it!"

The group erupted into accusations.

"Tough crowd," Benny whispered.

Oliver's first magic show was not shaping up to be a success.

MAYBE THE CAT'S ON A "BUSINESS TRIP."

DID YOU LOOK UNDER THE PATIO?

THE TWINS DID IT!

Maddox's mother did her best to change the mood of the party.

"Intermission!" she announced. "Why doesn't everyone go swimming? We'll have more magic in a bit. Be careful around the Candycano. It erupts every fifteen minutes."

The children turned around to see the fearsome Candycano. Sure, a lot of parties have candy tables, but this was a fancy party. It had a candy *volcano*. A towering mountain of sugary treats topped by a crater of melted chocolate lava.

Hanging above was an illuminated countdown clock.

Released from magic show prison, some kids made a break for the Candycano, some for the pool or climbing wall. Only Rose braved the reptile petting zoo.

"Not so fast, you three!" Maddox's mother said to Oliver, Bea, and Teenie. "I don't know what happened here, but my son thinks you stole his present."

Benny tugged on a strand of Oliver's hair. "Let's make a break for it, Ollie! Our gooses are cooked. Our hen has mislaid the golden egg. And the chickens have come home to roost. Know what I mean, kid?"

As usual, Oliver had no idea what Benny meant.

He also had no idea who stole the robo-cat, and it was clear that Maddox's mother expected some answers.

"Let the police sort it out," Maddox said.

The whole crew shuddered at the mention of police involvement, none more so than Benny.

Maddox's mother tried to ease the tension. "No, no, no, that won't be necessary. We'll just call their parents."

Now Bea and Teenie were even more terrified. If their fathers thought they'd stolen a robot, they'd be grounded for months, and their own birthday was just weeks away.

"Please don't call our dads!" Teenie cried.

"We'll get the cat back, we promise," Bea said. "Just give us a little time. Oliver will find it before his encore performance."

"I *will*?"

"Here—" Before Oliver could protest, Bea pulled out the rider and scribbled an addendum on her sister's back.

Maddox's mother read through the updated agreement and checked her watch. "Okay," she said. "You three have thirteen minutes—watch the Candycano clock—until Oliver's next performance. We'll expect the cat back by then. Does that sound good, Maddox?"

Magician's Rider

THE UNBELIEVABLE OLIVER

- Cake
  4 slices
  corner preferred

- Microphone & stand

- Sparkling Water
  (Room Temp!)

Addendum

- 2nd Performance pending solved mystery

"Sure, whatever," he said to his mother.

Just before Maddox snuck out the door, he whispered so only Oliver (and Benny) could hear, "If you don't find the cat, I'll make Joe beat you up."

As everyone knew, Joe, the biggest kid in the

third grade, did everything Maddox told him to. If he said to beat them up, then—

Bea and Maddox's mother shook hands, not realizing Maddox had just made his own secret amendment to the deal.

Our friends had thirteen minutes to solve the mystery. Or else. As for Benny, he was oddly silent, but Oliver's head felt suddenly very warm and very wet.

"Does anybody else want some candy?" asked Teenie.

INTERMISSION

I think it's a good time for us to take a break as well. May I suggest the bathroom? Or perhaps a chocolate chip cookie?

(Just please no cookies **in** the bathroom.)

See you in a few minutes.

The Who, the What, and the Where

A moment later, our three friends were huddling in the shadow of the Candycano.

After they'd had their fill of jelly beans and Skittles, but before they'd moved on to candy corn or Red Vines, Bea pulled out her notebook. Behind her, the Candycano gurgled ominously. Chocolate lava trickled down the sides—a warning of things to come.

The Mystery of the Missing Robo-Kitty, Bea wrote.

"Okay, here's the game," she said. "We're detectives and a robotic cat has been stolen."

"It's not a game," Oliver pointed out.

Bea looked at him as if he were being very silly. "Yeah, but the rules are the same."

Teenie nodded in agreement. "Rules are rules."

Oliver was getting worried. "I don't think we have any of those things."

"Darn! He's right," said Teenie. "Should we play Super Fairies instead?"

"Let's just summarize what we know so far," said Bea. "It all comes down to the Who, the

What, and the Where. For example, Ms. Peacock with the knife in the dining room. So—who are our suspects?"

"You, me, and Oliver," said Teenie quickly.

Bea wrote their names down under the heading *SUSPECTS*.

"But none of us did it," said Oliver, who was looking at the countdown clock and beginning to panic.

"Oliver, stop being so neg-
ative! Actually, that's a good
point," she admitted, cross-
ing out their names. "I'll be
the Who. My job will be to
look for new suspects."

"What am I looking for?"
Teenie asked.

"You're the What. The
weapon."

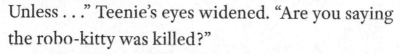

"But there isn't a weapon.
Unless . . ." Teenie's eyes widened. "Are you saying
the robo-kitty was killed?"

"No! I mean, I don't think so, but it *was* stolen,"
said Bea. "What was it stolen *with*? That's the
question. What do you need to move a robot?"

"A phone," said Oliver.

Bea glared at her friend. "If you won't help, at
least be silent."

"An app," said Teenie. "The robot runs on an
app!"

"Yes, that's it!" said Bea. "And for an app you need . . . a phone. So the weapon is a phone?"

"That's what I said," said Oliver.

"Don't gloat, Oliver. It's not nice. Teenie, your job will to be to look at people's phones for the RK-D2 app."

Teenie nodded gravely. "Those phones will never see me coming. A Super Fairy moves silently and cannot be seen." She demonstrated by hiding behind a potted palm tree.

Bea pointed to Oliver. "You're the Where."

THE WHERE
(The scene of the crime)

The Kitchen

Oliver

"Huh?"

"You investigate the crime scene. Maddox said the cat was last seen in the kitchen, right? Start there."

For Benny, who had been listening inside Oliver's hat, this was too much. "Crime scene?!" he whispered hoarsely. "We can't go there. Think! It's bound to be swarming with police."

Bea looked at Oliver askance. "Did you say 'swarming with fleas'? Maddox doesn't have any pets."

"No, I . . . Never mind, I'll go," said Oliver unhappily.

"Great," Bea said. "We'll meet back here in T-minus nine minutes. Everyone, synchronize your watches!"

None of them had watches, so the synchronizing went fast.

"Okay, go!"

Teenie ran off.

Bea buried her head in her notebook, leaving their reluctant fellow detectives, Oliver and Benny, to investigate the scene of the crime.

Now, please don't think Bea was shirking her own detective duties. It's true that there was a novel hidden inside her notebook, and, all right, she may have opened it and read a paragraph or two. But,

I promise, she quickly closed it and jumped into action.

Besides, reading a novel is an excellent way to investigate all sorts of things. Just think of all you're learning about detective work right now!

The Investigation, Part One

OLIVER: THE WHERE

THE WHERE
(The scene of the crime)

Oliver wasn't sure where the kitchen was, but he followed a caterer holding a near-empty tray of miniature churros.

"Grab me one of those, would ya?" Benny requested. "If I'm going on the lam again I need a full tummy."

"The lamb? Is there a lamb here?" asked Oliver. "I thought the petting zoo was all reptiles."

"*On the lam,* Ollie. On the run from the law."

"Oh."

"You're going to have to know the lingo if you're going to keep going to parties like this one."

The kitchen was bigger than Oliver's whole apartment. Maddox had said the robo-kitty went missing from the kitchen island, but there were *three* islands in the kitchen.

"A kitchen archipelago," Benny whispered. Oliver didn't know what *archipelago* meant, but it sounded scary. (It's a group of islands, if you're curious.)

"Well, what now, Ollie? You gonna dust for fingerprints?" the bunny asked.

Ollie looked around the kitchen in despair. Even if he knew how to dust for fingerprints, he wouldn't be able to; the islands were covered with catering equipment and piles of food.

"Get these out to section seven!"

Oliver didn't realize he was the one being shouted at until he was handed a tray of juice boxes. With his fancy jacket, he'd been mistaken for a waiter.

Oliver started to sweat. He didn't know how to investigate a crime scene, he didn't know how to be a waiter, he didn't know where section seven was, or even if he should accept tips.

Then he saw Joe, headed right toward him with a big trash bag.

"Out of my way!"

"What a nice young man, taking out the trash like that," Benny said, watching Joe go.

Oliver picked himself up, along with a few juice boxes. "Actually, maybe it's not nice to say so, but Joe's not nice at all."

"Huh, very suspicious." Benny scratched his own head and Oliver's at the same time. "Maybe you should investigate."

"You're right!" In his excitement, Oliver was about to run out of the kitchen. Then he realized he'd forgotten something. "Hey, Benny? How do you investigate?"

"Well, you want to trail that kid, right?" Benny jumped down, using the hat as a parachute. He reached back into the hat and grabbed a pair of sunglasses. "Did you bring a disguise?"

"I didn't even bring swim trunks."

"Kid, this is a pool party!" Benny shook his head. "Anyway, we'll have to be careful."

"'Course your best bet, to avoid being seen at all, is to run away," said Benny.

"I can't run away!" said Oliver. "What about Bea and Teenie!"

"You do what you want, but I gotta split. Those wise guys in Reno, they put a tail on me."

"You weren't born with one?"

"I'm talking about the fuzz, kid."

"Your tail's not fuzzy?" Now Oliver was really confused.

"My tail's plenty fuzzy, thank you very much! The fuzz are the police. You think those coppers are coming here for some kid's cat toy? I don't think so."

By now they were outside. Joe was nowhere to be seen.

"But I need your help finding Joe," Oliver said desperately. "Where would the garbage go?"

"How should I know? Do I look like a map?"

"The map! You sure are smart, Benny. And not just for a bunny." Oliver unfolded his party map.

"What are you saying—most bunnies are dumb?"

"No. No. Not at all! You'd be smart, no matter what kind of . . . small furry animal you were."

The rabbit looked as though he had a few choice furry words for Oliver. "I'll get you as far as the garbage. Then you're on your own, Ollie."

"Refuse and Recycling?" said Oliver, studying the map. "You think that means garbage?"

"Well, it don't mean roses."

(True. Unless you refuse roses. Then they become refuse, pronounced *REH-fuse*, as well. Personally, I always refuse roses, except when they come with chocolate.)

Now that Teenie and Oliver had gone, other kids were starting to come up to the Candycano for their sugar fix. Bea found that if she kept her nose in her notebook, they barely noticed that she was there, and they spoke freely amongst themselves. Maybe she would find her suspect just by standing still and listening!

After all, the Genius Fairies always said "Observation is the key to understanding." And eavesdropping is just observing with your ears, right?

Bea had always assumed that her classmates said clever and fascinating things when she wasn't around. Why else would they be so much more interested in each other than they were in her? But listening to them now she was forced to admit that she'd been wrong.

Here are some of the things she heard:

And so Bea learned an important lesson. While her classmates did all share a characteristic that she lacked, it wasn't that they were clever and fascinating. It was that they were all willing to do crazy, possibly dangerous things.

Alas, she was still no closer to identifying a suspect in the Case of the Missing Robo-Kitty.

Then something caught her eye: a red line snaking away from the Candycano. It was a licorice rope leading off into the distance. Why would someone leave good licorice on the ground and not eat it, she wondered.

Bea picked up the trail and followed the red rope around the Olympic-sized pool, under the lifeguard station, and into the bushes, eating the delicious evidence along the way.

TEENIE: THE WHAT

Meanwhile, Teenie was hopping around the yard, looking for a phone with the RK-D2 app.

She found Maddox's mother lying on a chaise by the pool, texting on her phone. Glancing over her shoulder, Teenie could see a text thread with Maddox's father.

(Normally, I do not encourage spying on people's texts, but I think we can agree that this was an exceptional circumstance.)

From the texts, Teenie learned how to operate all the TVs in the house, but that wasn't much help in their investigation.

As she passed the lifeguard stand, the lifeguard dropped his phone onto a towel and walked over to the edge of the pool to shout at a swimmer. Teenie judged she had two minutes to examine his phone. She grabbed it before the screen locked.

The lifeguard's phone was full of selfies. She didn't think he looked too great in any of them. Then again, maybe she wasn't a very good judge, she admitted to herself.

The only other picture was one of Oliver in a magic store, wearing his top hat. An odd coincidence, yes. But again, not very helpful.

Most of the other partygoers didn't have phones. Except Maddox, who'd left his on a rock when he went swimming. He must have been playing a game on the phone, because as soon as Teenie turned it on the screen was swarming with zombies.

"AAAAAAH!" Startled, she dropped the phone into a puddle.

Quickly, she wiped it off. Hopefully, there wouldn't be lasting damage.

Feeling a little discouraged, Teenie went back to the Candycano to look for her sister, but Bea was gone. A lot of candy was gone too. Fortunately, a lot more was still there. An entire mountain of candy, in fact.

After all that hard work, Teenie figured she deserved a short break and a sweet or two. A sour gummy. Some Skittles. She loved Skittles. Maybe a few cookies. According to the countdown clock she still had five minutes. Plenty of time to solve the case.

The Investigation, Part Two

OLIVER: THE WHERE, PART TWO

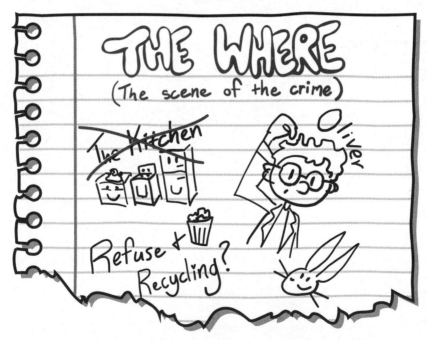

Holding his map open, Oliver walked around the house, toward the Refuse and Recycling area. Holding the top hat over his head, Benny followed as discreetly as he could.

As soon as they rounded the corner, they saw the trash bins. And there was Joe, up to his shoulders in the trash, looking for something. Oliver nudged Benny. "Hey, there he is!"

Benny looked up from under the brim of the hat and glanced nervously at their surroundings. "Keep it down!"

He nodded to the nearest trash bin. They ducked behind it and watched Joe, still digging in the trash.

"All right, we found him," said Benny. "Now it's time I hit the road."

Oliver looked down at his rabbit friend in distress. "Please don't go yet! What about the encore performance?"

"Sorry. It ain't only the cops, kid. I got dreams." The bunny reached into the top hat and pulled out a small piece of cardboard. It had a picture of the sun setting over a green farm. "See this—Kern County. That's where I'm headed. Time to settle down. Get a warren of my own. Someplace I can raise a small family of forty or fifty . . ."

No Essential Vitamins
Less Essential Minerals
Just Sodium

Kern County Farms

BOX TOPS 4
CORPORATIONS

Oliver examined the picture. "You know that's a cereal box top, right?"

Irritated, Benny snatched the cardboard back. "That don't mean the farm ain't real!"

Their argument was interrupted by a loud "MEOW!"

The robo-cat! Oliver thought, but just then, a large possum scurried from behind the bins.

Oliver frowned. "Benny, do possums meow?"

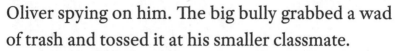

"Benny?" Oliver repeated.

Benny might not have heard the question, but Joe did. He spotted Oliver spying on him. The big bully grabbed a wad of trash and tossed it at his smaller classmate.

"Trying to steal the trash too, huh?" Joe sneered.

"Sorry, I was looking for the stolen robo-cat," said Oliver bravely. "Thought I heard a meow."

"No you didn't," Joe insisted. "You heard this!"

He dumped the remaining trash over Oliver's head, and walked away, having made his point.

Oliver wiped the garbage and a few tears from his eyes.

He knew what he had heard. Joe was hiding something. Something that walked and talked like a cat.

"I think we have our suspect, Benny," said Oliver in an excited whisper, while wiping off milky cereal. "The cat burglar is Joe!"

SUSPECT #1
Joe: the Muscle

"Except a cat burglar is actually a nighttime burglar, huh?" continued Oliver. "Not somebody who steals cats. But you know what I mean. Well, anyway . . . Why do you think he did it? You think he was jealous of Maddox maybe?"

Oliver glanced around, but he didn't see the rabbit. Or even the hat.

"Benny?"

He didn't get an answer because Benny was gone.

Still sticky and dripping cereal, Oliver checked all the obvious rabbit spots, like the vegetable garden and the salad bar, but he saw no furry white animals or even any roving top hats.

Three minutes left on the countdown clock, and still no sign of Benny.

Beginning to despair, Oliver glanced under the lifeguard tower, only to jump back in alarm when the lifeguard blew his whistle. Oliver looked up to see his cousin Spencer, who had traded in his magic store uniform for orange trunks and a life preserver.

Oliver was not especially surprised. Spencer was trying to buy a car, so he took any job he was qualified for—*and* any job that he was unqualified for.

"Spencer, have you seen a rabbit anywhere?"

"I'm on lifeguard duty," said Spencer with more than a trace of self-importance. "My eyes have been locked like laser beams on this pool. So unless your rabbit is a plastic flotation device . . . What happened to you, Oliver? You smell horrible. You should jump in the pool and clean up."

"But I don't have a swimsuit."

"Dude, this is a pool party!"

"That's what *he* said."

"Who?"

"Nobody."

Oliver wanted to keep searching for Benny, but Spencer blew his whistle a second time, causing Oliver to trip over a long red candy rope and fall right into the pool.

What would he do without Benny, Oliver wondered as he plunged deep underwater. A second ago, he was a triumphant detective. Now he was just another failed, sopping wet magician. There was no way he could perform without his rabbit partner.

BEA: THE WHO, PART TWO

THE WHO
(Suspects)

Bea didn't notice that she'd caused her friend to trip. She figured Oliver must have dived into the pool in search of clues.

Having followed the licorice rope as it snaked away from the Candycano, and wound around the pool and under the lifeguard tower, she now found herself nearing the end of her long red trail: the craft table.

At the craft table, Memphis sat alone, talking on a walkie-talkie.

Memphis had never seemed to be the crafty type. What was she doing there? And who was she talking to?

In front of Memphis was an elaborate castle that she was building from brightly colored plastic blocks. All over the table, she had spread diagrams and plans. None of which seemed to relate to the box that the blocks came in.

"That doesn't look like the castle on the box," said Bea, walking up.

Memphis put down a block. "This is more of a challenge."

"What is?" Bea asked. "What are you building?"

"Stop bothering me!" Memphis sneered. "Don't you and your sister have more presents to steal? And where's your dumb friend, the 'magician'?"

Bea eyed the block structure. Not only was Memphis not building the castle on the box, she wasn't building a castle at all. She was building a model of a large suburban house. Maddox's house.

As for the papers on the table, they included a map of Maddox's home, and the instructions for the RK-D2!

"Aha!" Bea exclaimed to herself, and made a note in her book.

SUSPECT #2

Memphis: the Brains

"Bye, Memphis!" she said cheerfully.

Then she trotted off to tell Teenie and Oliver about her discovery, eating the remaining licorice rope all the way back to the Candycano.

TEENIE: THE WHAT, PART TWO

Back at the Candycano, Teenie was still eating sweets. She ate:

Gummy bears

Gummy worms

Chocolate

Candy-coated chocolate

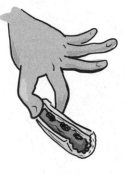

Candy-coated peanut butter

Peanut butter and celery with raisins (which had no business on the Candycano, but she ate it anyway)

Yogurt raisins (which she hated, but still had seven just to be sure)

All that candy had made her a little jumpy.

Actually, it had made her very jumpy. She leaped away from the table onto the diving board and straight over the deepest part of the pool and onto the other side.

With a loud whistle, the lifeguard shouted, "No jumping! Although I admit that was really cool!"

"Thanks!"

Teenie kept going past the Jacuzzi and DJ booth. She cartwheeled through the tennis court and hopped on one leg under the regulation basketball hoop. She walked on her hands through the cactus garden and scaled the climbing wall with her eyes closed. Finally, she arrived at the enormous bouncy castle.

Never had she felt a stronger urge to bounce.

Kicking her shoes off, she jumped right over the Slip 'N Slide moat and into the center of the castle. Jayden, Joe, and Maddox were already there, trying and failing to do flips. Teenie could do a double flip, backward *and* forward. She decided this was a perfect chance to show off.

"Hey, get out of here!" Maddox shouted. "You thief! I told your friend if you don't give back the cat, Joe will beat you up."

This was the first Teenie had heard about getting beaten up. Until now she'd thought the worse the day could get would be a call to her dads.

Joe didn't know about the planned assault either, but he took it in stride. "Yeah, get out of here before I beat you up."

"Besides, this bouncy castle is only regulated for . . ." Jayden calculated on his watch to be sure. "Three people."

"Yeah!" Joe agreed like always.

Teenie didn't think this was true. A massive inflatable birthday attraction like this one could easily hold a dozen more children. It had two floors, parapets, and even a dungeon.

Teenie started to protest, but Maddox stopped her. "Joe, get her out of here."

With that, Joe picked up Teenie and tossed her straight into the moat. She slid all around the castle

and back to the entrance, where the other children
had left their shoes.

Teenie counted five sets of sneakers, including
her own. While she was being tossed out they'd let
Memphis in without any questions. Teenie was fu-
rious.

She decided that the most sensible response was to tie their shoes together.

She started with Maddox's and Memphis's limited edition Air Mikes. Then moved on to Joe's rip-off version of the same shoes. Jayden's shoes didn't even have laces, but instead tightened with a mobile app. She'd have to use his phone, which was conveniently stuck inside his left shoe.

Teenie gasped as she picked up Jayden's phone. The screen lit up with the RK-D2 app.

"Aha!" she exclaimed.

Still shoeless, Teenie ran to tell Bea and Oliver how she'd cracked the case.

11

Rabbit, Run

Benny was feeling jittery. He didn't like possums, for the obvious reason 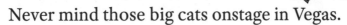 that possums are made out of nightmares and teeth. He didn't like cats either, to be honest, not even robotic ones. Never mind those big cats onstage in Vegas.

Boo!

And then there were the cops and who knew how many bounty hunters after him by this point. All because of one lousy bet. Could he be blamed for betting all his money on a horse named Turnip Thunder? Turnip was his favorite root vegetable!

Well, no more turnip for him. The only thing turned *ip*—or up—these days was the heat. And it was turned way, way up. If he ever wanted to get to Kern County, he'd have to start hopping. Fast.

First, he had to bust out of this party. But how? Half the backyard was taken up by the giant swimming pool. Rabbits don't swim. Period. And everywhere you looked, there were children. Screaming. Splashing. Whipping towels. It was a zoo.

He hopped a low fence and found himself in some sort of enclosed garden. Here it was unexpectedly peaceful. Only one kid. The girl with cat ears. She sat talking to what appeared to be a toad. They both seemed harmless enough. Unless the toad was about to turn into a prince, but that seemed unlikely.

Perhaps he should hunker down here for a bit? At least until the heat was off him? There was even some food and torn newspaper spread around the ground.

I could get used to this, Benny thought, piecing

together a sports page. (Even as a touring magician's rabbit, Benny had insisted that his bedding be changed daily, always with the latest sports page, for cleanliness—and for betting on horses.)

But something was wrong, he realized, looking at the ground more closely. The food wasn't for rabbits. Rabbits eat vegetables. Here it was all bugs. Crickets, worms, even ants.

This was no rabbit warren, that was certain.

A field mouse darted by.

"Say, buddy," Benny said. "Watch where you're going!"

The mouse, running at top speed, turned only to yell:

AHIYAAAAAARAAAAAH!

Sheesh, Benny thought.
Mice are so rude.

Benny had never much cared for mice, who were terrible magicians and worse comics. He'd take a dove over a mouse any day, and don't even get him started on doves.

He decided to investigate a little further.

Hat on his head, he hopped over a hollow log and a wobbly stack of stones, only to confront a plastic baby pool. Why a baby pool with such a large in-ground pool nearby?

Nothing made any sense until he saw an unwelcome sign:

Terrified, Benny landed in the baby pool, splashing the shallow water.

He was momentarily safe from the snake, but then a monitor lizard snuck out from behind a rock. The lizard's long tongue flicked in the air as the lizard clawed its way into the pool and approached our dear rabbit.

Benny scampered up the slide on the side of the pool and made a leap for a nearby rock. The rock was sloped and bumpy, and his feet slipped as he tried to catch hold. Just as he'd steadied himself, the rock rose in the air.

Because it wasn't a rock. It was a tortoise. A very old, very unhappy tortoise.

"Slow down, stranger," said the tortoise. "You think you can just hop a ride?"

"Ack!" Benny yelped. "You can talk?!"

"I'm 125 years old," the tortoise said, insulted. "I've learned a trick or two."

"125 and still performing for children's birthday parties," said Benny, sliding off. "Tough gig."

"Maybe so," said the tortoise, eyeing Benny's top hat. "That's one funny-looking shell you got there."

"Ha! That's a good one," said Benny, not meaning it. "You don't by chance know the way out of here, do you, old man?"

"Sure I do," said the tortoise.

The bunny waited, but the tortoise didn't say anything more.

"Well?" prompted Benny. "Where's the exit?"

"Far away."

"Where far away?"

The tortoise looked Benny up and down. He seemed to be weighing his desire not to help the rabbit against his desire for the rabbit to leave.

"A half day's journey to the north," he said finally, nodding across the small enclosure. "But a young hare like you should make it in half that time. Wanna race?"

"The Tortoise and the Hare, huh?" said Benny, already hopping away. "You're a real comedian."

He was home free. He would run out the back gate, down the alley, and over to a bus stop before the cops could even catch wise. In no time at all, he'd be on the five o'clock "Sunsetter" train to Kern County.

But just as he was about to make his final escape, the Candycano clock caught his eye. Two minutes until explosion. Meaning two minutes until show-time.

Showtime. The word flashed in his head like a Vegas marquee.

He'd never missed a show in his life. Even in the days when they were throwing tomatoes at him—and no, those tomatoes weren't for him to eat.

Could he really leave Oliver in the lurch? The boy's classmates were worse than a pack of wolves. They would eat Oliver alive.

The rabbit looked into the deep dark recesses of his hat and he knew what he had to do. The country life would have to wait a little longer. He was still a magician's rabbit, and a magician's rabbit never abandons his magician.

But how to get back to Oliver in time? There were snakes and swimming pools and a ridiculously large suburban backyard between them.

Just then he saw the girl with the cat ears petting a lizard. That girl had sucker written all over her. Swallowing his pride, Benny put on his best sad bunny face, and hopped on over.

He knew it was risky, catching a ride with a girl like Rose. No doubt she would pet his head, and talk to him as if he were her "wittle baby bunny." She might even—oh please no!—nuzzle his nose. It would be humiliating. But it was time to take one for the team.

He lived by one credo, and one credo only: The show must go on.

Alibis, Alibis, Alibis

Out of breath, Teenie ran back to the Candycano, only to find Oliver pacing back and forth, still soaking wet from the pool, and chomping through cake pops. Above him the countdown continued.

"Have you seen my rabbit?" he asked immediately.

"No," said Teenie. "But I know who did it! I know who the burglar is!"

"Oh, so do I," said Oliver, who was more concerned about Benny at the moment.

"And so do I!" said Bea, who had just arrived. She held her notebook in the air, excited to share her discovery. "I'll go first."

"No, I will!" said Teenie. "You always go first."

"That's not true—you do!"

Before the issue could be resolved, a red siren started whirling above the volcano, along with a swirl of cotton candy smoke. *Eruption in one minute,* noted the countdown clock.

"Well," said Maddox's mother, walking up to them with her son and his friends in tow. "Did you figure it out? Maddox wants his robotic dog back, and—"

"You mean cat!" several voices corrected her.

"Robotic *cat,* yes. And I must admit I'm very curious to find out what happened to it."

"We each figured it out by ourselves," Bea said proudly. "We know who stole the RK-D2!"

"Duh," Maddox replied. "You did."

"Nope," said Oliver.

"Nuh-uh," Bea said.

"No way," said Teenie.

They each took a deep breath and shouted:

Oliver, Bea, and Teenie looked at one another in surprise. They had identified three separate suspects: Memphis, Joe, and Jayden.

Maddox laughed. "You guys can't even get your stories straight."

"But I know it was Joe," Oliver said. "He took out the garbage and I heard it MEOW!"

Maddox rolled his eyes. "Joe does all my chores."

"What about Jayden?" Teenie said. "He had the RK-D2 app open on his phone."

"Ha!" Maddox said. "Jayden does all my homework. I gave him the app. I'm not going to learn some computer program just to play with a toy."

Jayden high-fived Maddox in what appeared to be agreement.

"Well, what about Memphis?" Bea said. "She had the instructions for the RK-D2, along with heist plans and a block model of the house."

"So? She does all my scheming for me. How am I supposed to prank my teachers with no one to plan it."

It seemed that Maddox had an excuse for everything. Bea made one last try.

"But why did she have the instructions for the RK-D2?"

"That's easy," Maddox explained. "Memphis does all of *Jayden's* homework."

Memphis nodded. "Besides, none of us could have taken that robot. We were all watching Oliver's stupid magic show."

"I'm afraid that's true," said Maddox's mom. "There must be another explanation."

THE WHO
(Suspects)
BEA is on the case!
(AKA me!)
①. ~~Joe~~
②. ~~Memphis~~
③. ~~Jayden~~
④. ~~Maddox~~

"But there's nobody else!" Bea wailed, looking down at her notebook. "All the possible suspects were at the show."

Maddox tilted his head toward Oliver, Bea, and Teenie. "You guys took the cat. And that's that."

He looked meaningfully at his friend Joe. "Remember what I said before?"

"Sure thing, boss." Joe eyed his three future victims as if they were tasty snacks. "I remember."

"Perhaps I should call your fathers after all," said Maddox's mother.

Oliver, Bea, and Teenie needed someone or something to save them fast.

"At least let Oliver do the magic show first!" said Bea, stalling.

At that moment, Rose approached holding an old magician's hat and a very squirmy rabbit.

"I've always wanted a rabbit," she said dreamily. "He's so soft and cuddly, but I could have sworn I heard him cursing."

"Benny, you're back!" Thrilled, Oliver held the rabbit and the hat to his heart.

"Yeah, and I almost got cuddled to death," Benny whined.

"Let's get this straight," he continued as Oliver quickly walked out of earshot of the others. "I do one more show, then I'm out. Bye-bye, kiddie pools and cat girls. Hello to my new warren and forty baby Bennys. Got that?"

"Okay, I got it! What trick are we going to start with?"

"Too bad you can't do a simple arrow catch," sighed Benny. "But under the circumstances, let's go straight to the Four Jacks. I'll walk you through it."

"The Four Jacks! Benny, you're a genius!"

"I've always thought so," said the rabbit modestly. "But you'd be surprised the prejudice some people have against rabbits."

"You solved the case!"

"The case? I like that . . ." mused Benny. "In a way, every magic show is a case. A mystery to be solved—"

"The *criminal* case."

Benny snorted. "You mean my gambling debts? Kid, it's gonna take more than a card trick to solve that one."

"No, I mean the robo—"

"Oliver!" Bea called out. "It's time for the show."

"You know, you look kind of crazy talking to yourself like that," Teenie whispered when he returned to the Candycano. "Couldn't you just, I don't know, *think* to yourself instead?"

Oliver was saved from responding when Bea shouted, "Watch out!"

Startled, Oliver fell backward into the volcano just as a chocolate geyser and a shower of sprinkles erupted from the top. He slid to the ground, looking like a hot fudge sundae.

The only things missing were whipped cream and a cherry.

13

The Four Jokers

A moment later, the party was reassembled for part two of the magic show, with Oliver, Bea, and Teenie standing onstage.

Not just Teenie, but all three of them were now bouncing with nervous energy. Oliver especially.

Still wet, he was trying to warm up.

"Listen, Ollie," whispered the rabbit in his ear. "Magic is make-believe, right? There's always a little storytelling involved. But with the Four Jacks, storytelling is everything."

"I told you, I only have four jokers," said Oliver under his breath.

"Call it the Four Jokers then," said Benny. "The point is, you need characters . . . atmosphere . . . suspense. And, of course, you need to know what's being stolen. You got something in mind?"

"Yep." That part he knew from the beginning.

"My go-to is carrots. Stolen carrots. It's a pun, see, because carats is how they measure diamonds. But I'm a rabbit, and rabbits eat—"

"I get it, Benny."

By now the crowd was getting a little restless. "Are you gonna start already?!" shouted Maddox.

"Just a second," said Bea.

"Magic takes time!" said Teenie.

They shot hurry-up looks at Oliver. In truth, they were getting antsy too.

"Okay, okay," he said.

Inside the hat, Benny prepared Oliver's deck of cards with the four jokers at the top. He handed them down to Oliver to show the crowd.

With Benny prompting him at every step, Oliver started telling the story of the Four Jokers.

"This trick takes place at a birthday party," Oliver began. "It was a big party. The whole third grade was invited—almost. But this wasn't a regular birthday party. It was also a robbery. The Four Jokers Robbery."

Oliver showed all four jokers to the audience, who now sat on the edge of their seats, their attention rapt. Being part of the birthday party, they were part of the story. Part of the magic.

Holding up the jokers one by one, he told the story of the robbery.

"The first joker was the muscle," Oliver announced, sliding a card to the bottom of the deck. "He did the heavy lifting. He took the birthday present and hid it under the garbage and out of sight."

Joe shifted in his seat. Because he was so big, the seat almost fell over.

"Now, the second joker." Oliver pulled another card from the top, then moved the card to the middle of the deck. "She stayed in the middle, acting as the brains. Giving instructions and making sure all details of the plan worked."

Memphis scanned the crowd to see if anyone looked her way.

"The third joker." Oliver held yet another card. "He was good at computers, a real technician. He programmed the robo-cat so they could sneak it out right under everyone's noses."

Jayden checked his phone as Oliver inserted the third card near the top of the deck.

"But here's the thing. None of those three could have done it alone. And that's why the plan was so good. Someone had to have stolen the birthday present in the first place."

Finally, Oliver revealed the fourth joker.

"The fourth joker. He stayed upstairs out of trouble, but he was the mastermind. He planned the robbery, and pinned it on this unsuspecting magician and his friends."

Maddox started to *boo!* but his mother shushed him.

"Once the coast was clear," Oliver continued, "the fourth joker called up all the other thieves."

Oliver kept one joker in his hand and then removed the top three cards of the deck. One by one, he revealed the other three jokers. It seemed as though they'd all magically traveled up through the deck.

"And then they got away with the stolen gift . . ." Oliver said.

Somehow, he'd pulled off the trick perfectly. Murmurs of "How'd he do that?" and "Wow!" spread throughout the audience.

Everyone stood and clapped. Everyone except Maddox, Memphis, Jayden, and Joe.

"Well, they almost got away," said Oliver.

Teenie and Bea looked at him in surprise. "Almost?"

"Almost," repeated Oliver. "The four jokers, or four *burglars,* they were Memphis, Jayden, Joe, and—"

"But it couldn't have been us, remember?" said Memphis, who was shifting nervously in her seat. "Everyone was right here."

"Yeah, we have alibis!" said Jayden.

"Right. That's why there had to be one more. And who was the fourth burglar?" Oliver paused, drawing out the suspense. "I'll give you a hint. It's his birthday."

"Maddox!" Bea shouted, finally figuring it all out and making a last note in her book.

"Right! Maddox is the fourth joker—I mean, burglar!" Teenie exclaimed. "He was the only one missing, so he's the only one who could have taken the RK-D2."

Almost everyone gasped and burst into applause.

And with the applause came the housekeeper holding the birthday cake. It was the biggest cake Oliver had ever seen. He started clapping as well— for the cake.

The Middle Name Drop

"Would you explain it all again?" Maddox's mom asked Oliver. "Slowly this time."

With the accusation and the cake, the party had come to a close. Each guest went home with a gift bag, a toy of their choice, and a promise not to repeat anything they'd seen or heard.

Now the four burglars, along with Oliver, Teenie, and Maddox's mom, were gathered around the living room's conversation pit.

"It's simple," said Oliver, his mouth half-full with his third slice of cake. "The four jokers were at the top of the deck the whole time. I just hid three random cards behind the first joker and used those instead."

"Not the trick," Maddox's mother clarified, although she was glad to know how he'd performed the trick, as it had been bothering her. "The crime."

"Oh. Um . . ." Oliver wanted to explain, but he'd just taken another bite of cake.

Luckily, Bea was paying attention. She opened her notebook.

"When Maddox went upstairs with the RK-D2, he didn't play with it, he put it in the trash," she explained. "Then Joe took the trash with the cat secretly inside. Meanwhile, Memphis monitored the whole operation, telling everyone what to do

when. And Jayden used the app on his phone to make the RK-D2 go where they wanted it to."

"Well . . ." Maddox's mother was still confused. "Then where's the cat now?"

"Check Jayden's phone," said Teenie.

Jayden resisted at first, but then handed his phone over to Maddox's mom. She put on her reading glasses to look at the app.

"Do any of you know how to work this thing?"

Jayden raised his hand, but Teenie took the phone and showed Maddox's mom how it worked.

"You just press this button here. That tells the cat it's dinnertime. She should come back to the phone right away."

From around the corner, they heard a meow.

Which sounded just like the possum from earlier, Oliver thought. The cat purred as it approached the phone.

With the RK-D2's return, all the evidence was on the table.

Maddox's mom finally showed her anger.

"Maddox Mortimer Marmor!"

The other children all gasped.

"She used his middle name!" Memphis whispered to Jayden, who was too shocked by the day's events to hear.

Spencer, who had just walked in from the pool, tiptoed out again. He didn't want any part of the fury coming after a middle name drop.

"You need to apologize to Oliver, Bea, and Teenie this instant," said Maddox's mother.

Maddox refused. "It wasn't my idea, it was the clown's!"

"Yeah," Memphis joined in. "He said he'd cut us in on the proceeds."

"The clown?" Maddox's mother had tried to

forget the clown from earlier. Whenever possible, it's best to not think about clowns for too long.

Spencer stepped back into the room. Despite the drama, he had to get paid.

"Hey, Mrs. M," Spencer said. "Do you have that check for me?"

"Yes, of course, dear." Maddox's mother forced a smile. "Here you go. Oh, and here's your check too, Oliver. You earned it."

Oliver and Spencer both smiled at their checks. Though Oliver had no idea what to do with a check. He supposed it would fit in his piggy bank.

"Thanks, Mrs. M," Spencer said. "But hey, that wasn't really a clown earlier."

This information came as a surprise to nearly everyone. He'd certainly looked like a clown. But then Oliver realized who it was.

"It was the Great Zoocheeni!" Oliver said at the same time as Spencer.

"Yeah," Spencer added. "How did you not notice? He still had his cape on."

Clearly, Oliver had a long way to go as both a magician and a detective.

"But why was he here?" Maddox's mother asked. "We'd already booked a magician."

"He didn't like anyone stepping on his turf," Spencer explained. "Zoocheeni told me 'That Oliver kid has another think coming! I'll show him.' Then he laughed like, 'AAHAHAHAHAHA-HAHAHAHAHAHAHAHAHAHAHAHA!' I think he wants all the birthday business for himself."

Almost as if called by name, the Great Zoocheeni burst into the room. He and his dove, Paloma, were both back in their traditional magician costumes.

"Grab that cat," Zoocheeni said, sending the dove toward the RK-D2. At first, he didn't notice the people around the kitchen table.

"Oh, hello, everyone. It is I, the Great Zoocheeni. I heard your magician was a total disaster, and a burglar to boot. And I have come to save the day."

Zoocheeni waited for applause, but nobody clapped. Spencer, seeing this was going to be an actual disaster, whistled out the door.

"Listen, clown, or Zoo-whoever," Maddox's mom said, still angry. "You need to leave immediately."

"Wait, Mom!" Maddox said. "He hasn't given me my money yet."

"And he won't!" She stood up. "You are in such trouble, young man. Wait till your father gets back from his business trip in a month."

Zoocheeni wiped his brow and said, "Phew." He had no intention of paying the children, and was glad to be let off the hook for the debt.

"Well, he still owes *us* money," Memphis said.

"He told us he would wire it," said Jayden.

"Yeah," Joe agreed.

The three bullies pounced on the magician. Seeing this was not going as planned, Zoocheeni moved to disappear.

"I'll just show myself out," Zoocheeni said. With a burst of smoke, he attempted to escape with grace and mystery.

The Great Zoocheeni took one step out the door, but tripped over an unlucky rabbit's foot. Benny put on his cutest, most innocent bunny face as the magician fell.

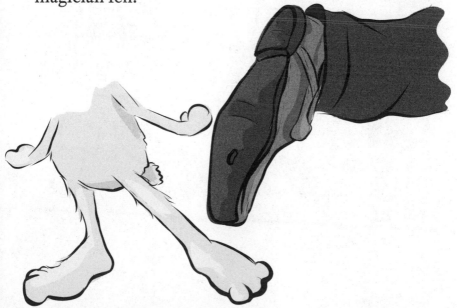

Jayden grabbed his phone from the table and took radio control over the RK-D2. The robotic cat swiped at the magician's dove. Paloma let out a startled "CAW! CAW!" and flew after her owner.

Memphis and Joe picked Zoocheeni off the ground and tossed him to the curb as Jayden and the RK-D2 chased Paloma along with him.

Only Oliver and the twins were left at the table with Maddox and his mother.

"Great party," Oliver said. "Is there any cake left?"

The After Party

The twins and Oliver left the party with goodie bags, cake, the RK-D2, and everything they could carry from the Candycano.

Back at the twins' apartment, they spread the loot out on the table. It was like Halloween. Only this time they didn't have to share with the twins' dads.

Benny used his teeth to open another whole bag of circus peanuts.

"Your rabbit seems really smart," Bea told Oliver.

Benny took a bow and then belched. He'd eaten a tremendous amount of circus peanuts. Feeling like he might be sick, the rabbit nodded to everyone, then hopped off the table.

"Where's he going?" Teenie asked.

"To the bathroom, I think," Oliver said.

"Is he potty-trained?" Bea asked. "He can use Calico's litter box."

"You mean *Frida's*," said Teenie.

Frida/Calico did not seem to like this idea or the rabbit who had invaded her space. She was already unhappy with the robotic cat taking her place. She let out an unkind *HISSS*.

For his part, Benny waved his fluffy tail back at the cat, then shut the bathroom door.

After a moment the toilet flushed.

"Wow," Bea said. "That *is* a well-trained rabbit. Great job, Oliver. We can't get our cat to do that."

Frida/Calico looked offended, but the twins didn't notice. She turned to her new robot "friend" for help. The robot wasn't much help.

"Your magic show was amazing, Oliver," Teenie said. "You learned all those tricks and figured out the whole heist and everything."

"You're like a genius," Bea added.

"He's more like a Super Fairy," Teenie corrected her sister.

"And your jacket even fits now," said Bea. "It must have shrunk from getting wet."

Oliver didn't know what to say. He was never very good at receiving compliments—mostly because he'd never received any.

"Thank you," Oliver said with a gulp. "I guess I did do a pretty good job. But I didn't figure it all out on my own. I couldn't have done it without Ben—"

Back from the bathroom, Benny gave Oliver a look. As much as he liked taking credit, the rabbit did not want to blow his cover.

"I mean, I couldn't have done it without you, Beatriz and Martina," said Oliver quickly.

Glad to be included, the twins clinked their empty teacups together.

"To the Unbelievable Oliver," Teenie said.

"And his assistants!" Bea added. "Bea and Teenie and Bunny."

"It's Benny," corrected Oliver. "Nothing bunny about it."

THE END

Thank you for reading!

ENCORE

How to Perform Oliver's Card Trick

Have you ever wanted to stage a robbery—or even just a card trick? Here's how to perform the trick called THE FOUR BURGLARS (also known as THE FOUR JACKS). The trick sounds a bit complicated, I admit, but with a little practice it becomes quite simple.

NEEDS:

—One deck of playing cards

—Two hands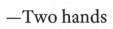

—A table or similar surface

—An audience (For example, a younger sibling or support-ive parent. Older siblings and unsupportive parents not rec-ommended.)

NOTE:

To perform the trick with four jokers, as Oliver does, you'll need to take two jokers from a spare deck of cards and add them to your deck. (Most decks include only two jokers.) Otherwise, go the traditional route and use four jacks or four kings. Or if you prefer female burglars, four queens. In fact, you can use four of any card you like. If you consider the number seven to be a thievish sort of number, then by all means make your four burglars out of four sevens.

← BURGLAR
7

BEFORE YOU PERFORM:

Hide backstage. Backstage is anywhere your audience can't see you. Like inside a closet, under a table, or behind the curtains. Remember, you are not hiding because you are nervous; you are hiding because you have to prepare your deck of cards.

PAY NO ATTENTION TO THE KID BEHIND THE CURTAIN.

To prepare your deck, first remove the four jacks, or four sevens, or four of whatever card you like (SEE ABOVE). These four cards are your BUR-GLARS. Then remove the top three cards from the deck. These cards are your DUMMIES. Place the three dummies above the four burglars, all cards facedown.

Hold these seven cards in your left hand. Be careful to hold them square so that nobody can see how many cards you have.

Grasping the rest of the deck with your right hand, bravely go out on stage and place the deck facedown on a table.

THE PERFORMANCE:

Still holding the remaining seven cards, begin telling your captive audience the Tale of the Four Burglars: "Once upon a time, there were four jacks [or sevens, etc.] who fell on hard times, so they decided to rob a . . ." In this book, the four burglars rob a birthday party. Usually, magicians have their burglars rob a bank. You could have yours rob a candy store, a house, or an arcade—but *never* a bookstore or magic shop! Make the robbery your own.

As you introduce them, briefly show the four burglar cards to the audience. But do not reveal the three dummy cards hidden behind the burglars! The dummies are your secret.

Four Jacks

Three Dummy Cards

Then place all seven cards (which your audience believes to be only four) facedown on top of the rest of the deck. Tell the audience that the deck is your bank or candy store or whatever building it is you want to rob.

Now it's time for the robbery.

BURGLAR #1

Explain that the job of the first burglar is to go down to the basement of the building and disable the security cameras. Without letting anyone see the face of the card, pick up the top card from the deck and insert it near the bottom of the deck. In reality, you are moving one of the secret dummy cards, not a burglar card, but as far as the audience knows it is a genuine burglar.

BURGLAR #2

The job of the second burglar is to create a disturbance in the lobby. (This is a good time for a fake fart noise, if you have it in you.) As you tell the audience about the second burglar, pick up the next card from the top of the deck and place it somewhere near the middle of the deck. Again, be careful not to show the face of the card because it's just a dummy.

BURGLAR #3

The third burglar is supposed to open the vault but instead heads upstairs to go to the bathroom. ("When you've gotta go, you've gotta go.") Or for some other reason you invent. To demonstrate, place the third card near the top of the deck. Do you let the audience see the card as you move it? No, of course not. You're not the dummy; the card is.

BURGLAR #4

The final burglar is the lookout. He or she stays on the roof to watch for police or superheroes or angry parents or whoever the burglars are afraid of—be creative. As you pick up this final card, do you show it to your audience? Sorry, trick question. The answer is yes, you do. Because it's one of the *real* burglar cards. (The three dummy cards have all been moved.) After everyone has seen the last burglar, put the card back on top of the deck.

Now comes the fun part. Trouble is on the way. Police sirens. Caped crusaders. Whatever and whoever you like.

Uh-oh. The lookout sounds the alarm: Tap three times on the top of the deck of cards and make a loud wolf whistle. If you can't whistle, just shout "ABRACADABRA!" or another magic word. This is the signal for all the burglars to come up to the roof.

Time for the big reveal. One by one, flip over the four cards on the top of the deck.

Since the three dummy cards are gone, all four burglars are now on top. To the audience, it looks as though they've magically risen through the deck.

To end your story, tell your audience that the burglars escape in a helicopter. Or maybe they hang-glide off the roof. In any case, let the cards flip in the air.

You've outsmarted your audience. And the bank.

At this point, you'll need to pause for applause.